PROTECTING LAND

BY DARLENE R. STILLE

The Child's World®

Published by The Child's World®
1980 Lookout Drive • Mankato, MN 56003-1705
800-599-READ • www.childsworld.com

PHOTO CREDITS
Stephen Haas/AP Images, cover, 1; J.L. Levy/Shutterstock Images, 5;
Amy Johansson/Shutterstock Images, 7; René Mansi/iStockphoto, 9;
Sophia Winters/Fotolia, 11; Alexey Stiop/Shutterstock Images, 13;
Volodymyr Krasyuk/Shutterstock Images, 15; Rob Mattingley/
iStockphoto, 17; Shutterstock Images, 19; Fotolia, 21; iStockphoto, 23;
Sven Hoppe/Shutterstock Images, 25; Aida Ricciardiello/Fotolia, 27;
Zeljko Radojko/Shutterstock Images, 29

CONTENT CONSULTANT
Mark C. Andersen, professor of fish, wildlife, and conservation ecology,
New Mexico State University

ACKNOWLEDGMENTS
The Child's World®: Mary Berendes, Publishing Director
The Design Lab: Design
Red Line Editorial: Editorial direction

ISBN: 978-1-60973-175-5
LCCN: 2011927674

Printed in the United States of America in Mankato, MN
July, 2011
PA02090

TABLE OF CONTENTS

Thick forests and quiet **wetlands** make up **wilderness** areas. Many countries try to protect wilderness lands by making them into national parks or forests. Governments own these lands and set rules about how the land can be used.

Saving trees is an important part of protecting land. The roots of trees can help keep soil from washing away. The leaves that fall to the ground provide nutrition to the soil and smaller plants. Trees give off oxygen, a gas in air that humans and animals need to breathe. Trees take in carbon dioxide, which is a **greenhouse gas**. Carbon dioxide

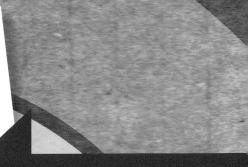

Protecting the trees in forests, such as the Superior National Forest in Minnesota, helps animals, soil, and humans.

traps heat energy from the sun and causes **global warming**.

Land must also be protected from pollution. Rain that falls on garbage can pollute the soil, lakes, and streams. Chemicals that kill weeds and pests can pollute soil as well.

Protecting land begins with you. And there are many ways that you can help.

MAKE A COMPOST BIN

If you have a backyard at your home, set aside a place to make a compost pile. Toss in food scraps and plant material. Orange peels, leftover veggies, grass clippings, dead leaves, and twigs are great for making compost. Water your compost every so often to keep it moist. In about six months to a year, you will have dark, crumbly soil. Spread it over garden plants and watch them grow!

WHY?

Compost helps useful bacteria and fungi grow. These bacteria and fungi break down the organic matter in your compost to create humus. Humus is the part of soil that is filled with nutrients. The more nutrients in your soil, the better the plants in your garden will grow.

Collect leaves and twigs for a compost pile.

TIP #2

GIVE FUNNY PRESENTS

Think of creative ways to wrap presents for birthdays and other holidays. For example, the Sunday comics make great gift wrap. It is colorful, and your friends and family members can also get a laugh.

WHY?

During the December holiday season, Americans throw away 4 million tons (3.6 t) of wrapping paper and shopping bags. Where does the wrapping paper come from? It comes from paper mills that use materials from trees. About 900 million trees are cut down each year and sent to US paper and pulp mills.

When you use old newspapers to wrap gifts, you'll help stop more trees from being cut down for wrapping paper.

PAPER OR PLASTIC?

What's the best answer when the checkout clerk asks if you'd like paper or plastic? "Neither one." Take your own cloth bag when you go shopping or use your backpack. Have the clerk put your groceries in your reusable bag.

WHY?

Grocery stores in the United States give out about 10 billion paper bags each year. A busy store uses about 700 bags an hour, which is the number of bags that can be made from one tree. Plastic bags, made from oil, take a long time to break down. A plastic bag dumped into a landfill will stay there for up to 1,000 years. As it breaks down, the plastic becomes smaller and smaller poisonous particles.

Using reusable bags when shopping helps reduce paper and plastic waste.

SPONSOR A WILD PLACE

Suggest that your class sponsor a wild place, such as the Arctic National Wildlife Refuge or Grand Canyon National Park, through the Sierra Club. The Sierra Club is the oldest **conservation** group in the Unites States. You can sponsor a wild place for as little as $20. Have a bake sale or collect pennies to raise the money.

WHY?

There are about 50 conservation groups in the United States. Some, such as the Sierra Club and Nature Conservancy, protect all kinds of lands. Other groups focus on protecting certain types of land, such as forests or coastlines. Others work toward protecting land in one state. Find a group that interests you, and join up!

When you sponsor a wild place, such as the Grand Canyon National Park, the money you donate goes toward conservation.

CHILDREN'S RAINFOREST

In the late 1980s, schoolchildren in Sweden sparked a movement to buy and care for endangered rainforest land in Costa Rica. After learning about this beautiful endangered land, they raised money by putting on plays and holding bake sales. They worked with people in Costa Rica to form the Monteverde Conservation League. There are now at least 55,600 acres (22,501 ha) of protected forests in Costa Rica.

MAKE JAR GARDENS

Collect small jars ranging in size from baby food jars to peanut butter jars. Wash the jars and remove the labels. Keep the lids. Gather together green-colored clay or play dough, glue, and small artificial flowers. Use a rolling pin to make the clay or play dough into a flat sheet. Use the mouth of the jar to cut out a circle of clay or dough. Glue it into the lid. Make a flower arrangement by sticking the flowers into the clay. Carefully put the jar over your garden and screw the lid on.

WHY?

You might see a glass jar or plastic bottle and think *recycle!* Reusing things is another way to keep trash out of landfills or garbage dumps. Making jar gardens is one way to reuse jars. They make nice gifts for Mother's Day, Father's Day, or any special holiday.

Clean out and reuse old jars of all sizes for creative and fun craft projects.

START A WEED PATROL

Dandelions might look pretty to you. But they are actually weeds that can take over a lawn. Get some friends together and arm yourselves with garden tools for pulling out weeds. Go on a hunt for dandelions and dig them out of the yard. Ask your neighbors if you can take the weeds out of their lawns, too!

WHY?

Chemical weed killers usually get rid of weeds. But they also put harmful chemicals into the soil. When it rains, the chemicals wash into drains. Chemicals washing off thousands of lawns in a city can dump a lot of poisons into the environment.

Pull weeds by hand instead of using harmful chemical weed killers on lawns.

SEND E-VITES AND E-CARDS

You can use a computer to make and send some really cool e-cards. You'll save some trees, too. Find Web sites that let you create and send e-vites and e-cards. You can even find sites that let you send your friends greeting cards that sing and dance.

WHY?

Many environmentalists say people should print less paper. About 7 billion greeting cards are sold each year in the United States. That is a lot of paper that could be saved!

Happy Mother's Day

By sending an e-card, you'll prevent a paper card from going into the garbage.

PLANT A TREE

One of the simplest and best things you can do for Earth is plant a tree. Find a space in a park or in your yard where there is soil and sunlight. Push a tree seed about an inch down in the soil and cover it up. Make sure to water it each day. Soon your tree will sprout aboveground.

WHY?

Trees have been called "the lungs of the planet." Trees "breathe" in carbon dioxide. They use this gas with water and sunlight to make their own food. Just by living, trees help stop Earth from becoming too warm. Trees "exhale" oxygen. This is the gas humans and animals need to breathe.

Planting and taking care of a tree is a great way to give back to Earth.

CHAMPION RECYCLER

Jack Potter, an 11-year-old from Iowa, collected almost 1,000 plastic bottle caps. He encouraged his community to recycle bottle caps, too. Jack earned the opportunity to make his recycling project an exhibit at the Iowa State Fair.

THINK OUTSIDE THE CEREAL BOX

Make picture frames for your photos or drawings from empty cardboard cereal boxes. Have an adult help you cut out the front and back of the box. Glue your picture to one piece of cardboard. Cut an opening in the other piece to fit your picture and attach it with glue. Decorate your frame by coloring it or gluing on pieces of cloth, tiny shells, or anything else that you like.

WHY?

Every American uses an average of 360 pounds (163 kg) of paper and cardboard each year. Recycling just what is used in cereal boxes means less waste in landfills.

Cut and decorate empty cereal boxes to make them into frames or other fun crafts.

USE VINEGAR ON WEEDS

Some weeds are just too tough to pull out. Or they keep growing back. Instead of spraying chemicals on them, spray vinegar. The acid in vinegar acts as a natural weed killer. Be careful not to spill the vinegar on other plants. It can kill flowers and grasses, too.

WHY?

Chemicals used to kill weeds on farms and lawns harm the land. Materials used to make chemical fertilizers are often scraped from mines. This process leaves ugly scars on the land. Chemical fertilizers seep into the soil and run off into lakes and streams. The chemicals can harm or kill fish and other creatures in the water.

Fill a spray bottle with vinegar to get rid of weeds without using harmful chemicals.

TIP #11

TAKE A LUNCH BOX TO SCHOOL

When you bring your lunch to school, pack your sandwich and other food in a metal or plastic lunch box. Put your lunch items into reusable containers. You will help the environment and keep your food fresher. And, your sandwich won't get squished!

WHY?

Many people are concerned that millions of plastic grocery bags can affect the environment. What about plastic sandwich bags? A family of five people uses up to 2,400 plastic sandwich bags each year. Very few sandwich bags get recycled. Sandwich bags used for school lunches account for more than 20 million of the sandwich bags that end up in US landfills.

Use plastic containers for your lunches instead of plastic bags.

MAKE A MINI-WETLAND

If you have a backyard that has clay or heavy soil, you can turn a small area into a wetland. Find the lowest spot. You may want to dig out some soil to make your wetland deeper. Then stop mowing the area. Water it often to keep the soil very wet. Then watch tall grasses and other plants grow. Soon you may see frogs, toads, and other small animals that live in wetlands.

WHY?

Wetlands are important environments. Swamps, marshes, and bogs are home to animals such as alligators and birds. Many animals that live in wetlands are endangered species. That's because many wetlands have been destroyed. The United States and other countries now have laws that protect wetlands.

In your yard, create a mini version of a wetland where grass, plants, and animals can make a home.

MORE WAYS TO GO GREEN

1. **Plant** tomatoes or peppers in a flowerpot garden.

2. **Turn** a cardboard box into a dollhouse by cutting out doors and windows and painting the box. Reusing cardboard saves space in landfills.

3. **Make** a jigsaw puzzle out of a cardboard pizza box.

4. **Save** gift boxes, gift wrap, and bows to reuse for wrapping presents.

5. **If** you only use one side of a sheet of paper when drawing or writing a note, save the paper and use the other side for scratch paper.

6. **Don't** litter parks or roadsides with trash. Instead, throw candy wrappers, paper cups, and other trash in a trashcan.

7. **Get** a library card and check out books instead of buying your own copies. Printing fewer books means using less paper and cutting down fewer trees.

8. **Use** a dishcloth or sponge instead of a paper towel to wipe up spills.

9. **Buy** products with the least amount of packaging, such as one big bag of chips instead smaller individual serving bags. The less packaging, the less garbage ends up in landfills.

10. **Buy** products made from recycled paper and other recycled materials.

11. **Find** out where you can take used batteries to recycle them. Batteries dumped into landfills can leak mercury, a deadly poison.

12. **Make** a poster showing why wetlands are important. Ask if you can hang it in your classroom or a public office.

13. **Write** a skit about a group of kids who decide to find ways to save tropical rainforests. Act it out for your classmates or family.

conservation (kon-sur-VAY-shun): Conservation is the preservation of the natural world. Some organizations work for the conservation of land.

endangered (en-DAYN-jurd): If something is endangered, it is in danger of dying out. Many people work to protect endangered forests.

global warming (GLOHB-ul WOR-ming): Global warming is the heating up of Earth's atmosphere and oceans due to air pollution. More trees on Earth can help stop global warming.

greenhouse gas (GREEN-houss GASS): A greenhouse gas is a gas like carbon dioxide or methane that helps hold heat in the atmosphere. Fewer trees lead to more greenhouse gas in the air.

wetlands (WET-lands): Wetlands are lands that are mostly underwater and have soggy soil. You can get a group of friends together to make wetlands in each other's yards.

wilderness (WIL-dur-niss): Wilderness is land that has its original characteristics, with minimal impact from humans. National parks and forests protect wilderness.

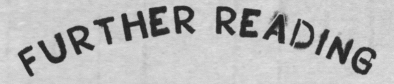

FURTHER READING

BOOKS

Greeley, August. *Fading Forests: The Destruction of Our Rainforests.* New York: PowerKids Press, 2003.

Latham, Donna. *Garbage: Investigate What Happens When You Throw It Out with 25 Projects.* White River Junction, VT: Nomad Press, 2011.

Simon, Seymour. *Tropical Rainforests.* New York: HarperCollins, 2010.

Slade, Suzanne. *What Can We Do about Pollution?* New York: PowerKids Press, 2010.

WEB SITES

Visit our Web site for links about protecting land:
http://www.childsworld.com/links

Note to Parents, Teachers, and Librarians: We routinely verify our Web links to make sure they are safe and active sites. So encourage your readers to check them out!

INDEX